THERE WAS AN OLD LADY WHO SWALLOWED A BELL!

by Lucille Colandro
Illustrated by Jared Lee

Cartwheel
·B·O·O·K·S·®

SCHOLASTIC INC.

New York   Toronto   London   Auckland   Sydney
Mexico City   New Delhi   Hong Kong   Buenos Aires

For Marietta and Mia, who love Christmas
— L.C.

To Ginger Estepp,
longtime dedicated associate
— J.L.

ISBN-13: 978-0-545-11098-3
ISBN-10: 0-545-11098-X

Text copyright © 2006 by Lucille Santarelli.
Illustrations copyright © 2006 by Jared D. Lee, Studio, Inc.
All rights reserved. Published by Scholastic Inc.
SCHOLASTIC, CARTWHEEL BOOKS, and associated logos are trademarks
and/or registered trademarks of Scholastic Inc.

10 9 8 7 6 5 4 3 2 1   8 9 10 11 12/0

Printed in the U.S.A.
This edition first printing, October 2008

There was an old lady who swallowed a bell.
How it jingled and jangled and tickled, as well!
I don't know why she swallowed a bell.
I wish she'd tell.

There was an old lady who swallowed some bows.
Soft as the snow, were those velvety bows.

She swallowed the bows to tie up the bell
that jingled and jangled and tickled, as well!

I don't know why she swallowed a bell.
I wish she'd tell.

There was an old lady who swallowed some gifts.
It gave her a lift to swallow the gifts.

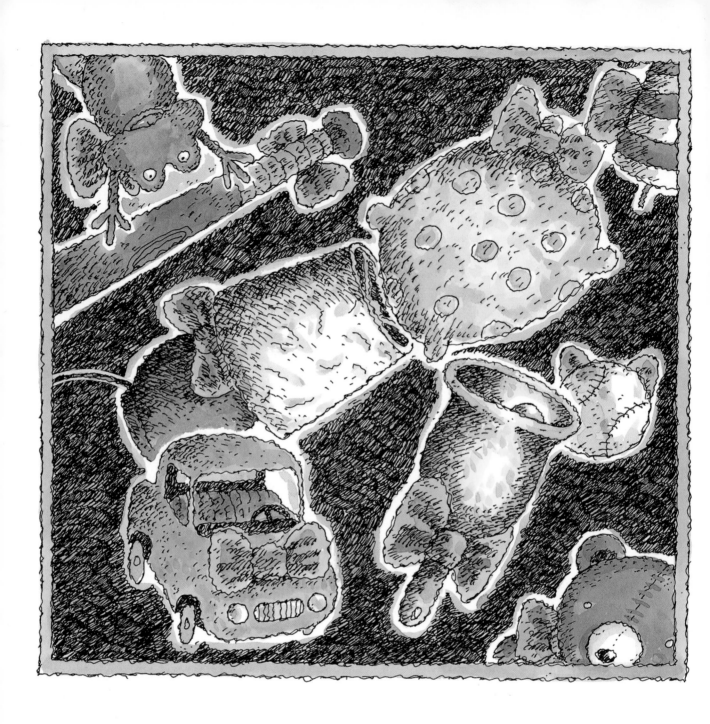

She swallowed the gifts to go with the bows.
She swallowed the bows to tie up the bell
that jingled and jangled and tickled, as well!
I don't know why she swallowed a bell. I wish she'd tell.

There was an old lady who swallowed a sack.
It was easy to pack—a very big sack.

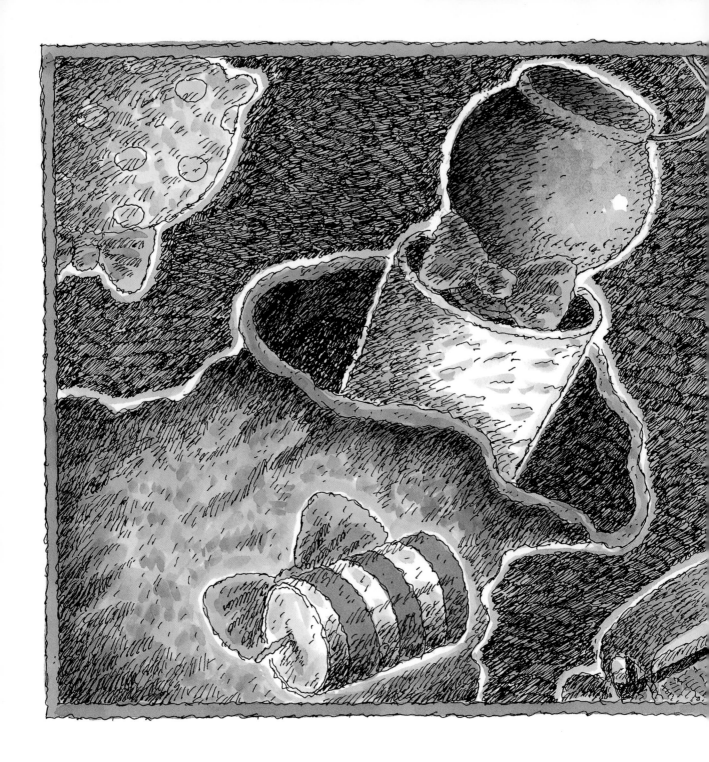

She swallowed the sack to hold all the gifts.
She swallowed the gifts to go with the bows.

She swallowed the bows to tie up the bell
that jingled and jangled and tickled, as well!
I don't know why she swallowed a bell. I wish she'd tell.

There was an old lady who swallowed a sleigh.
What a ton it weighed, that shiny red sleigh!

She swallowed the sleigh to carry the sack.

She swallowed the sack to hold all the gifts.

She swallowed the gifts to go with the bows.
She swallowed the bows to tie up the bell
that jingled and jangled and tickled, as well!

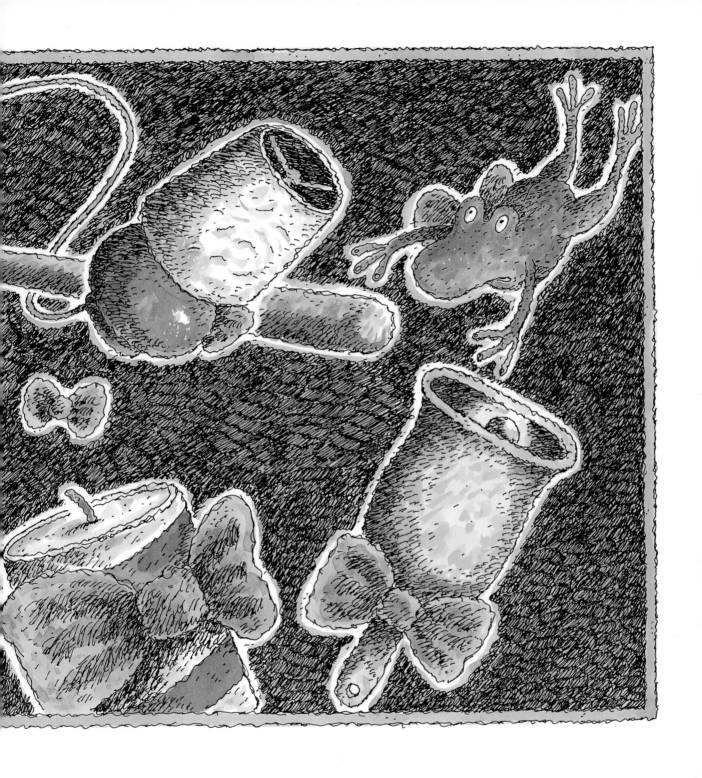

I don't know why she swallowed a bell.
I wish she'd tell.

There was an old lady who swallowed some reindeer.
They were in full flight gear, those soaring reindeer.

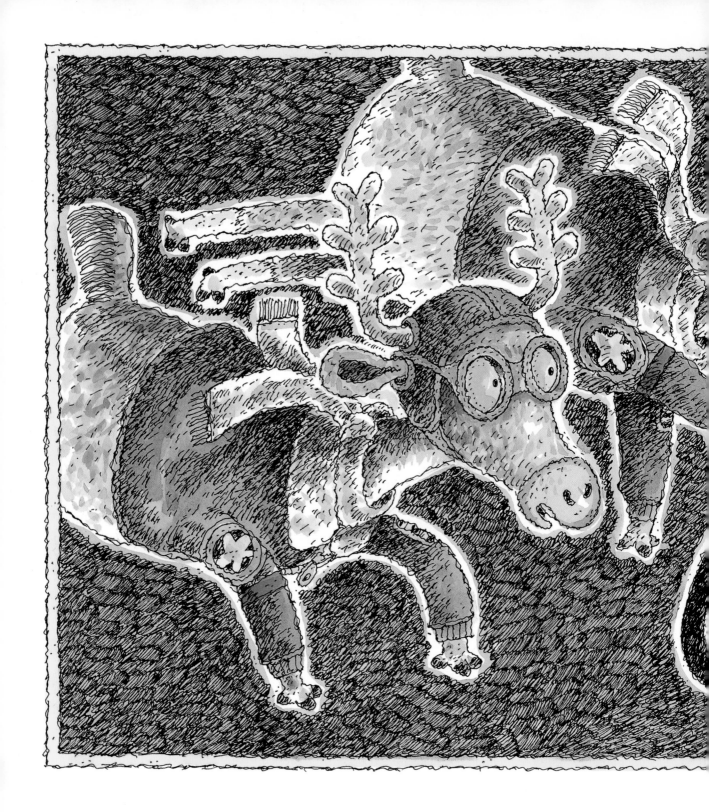

She swallowed the reindeer to steer the sleigh.

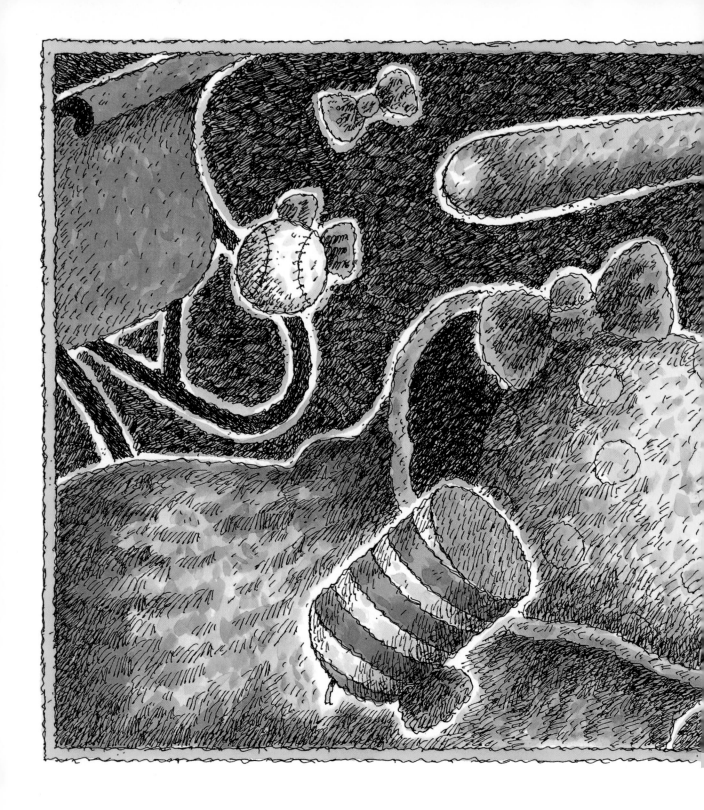

She swallowed the sleigh to carry the sack.

She swallowed the sack to hold all the gifts.

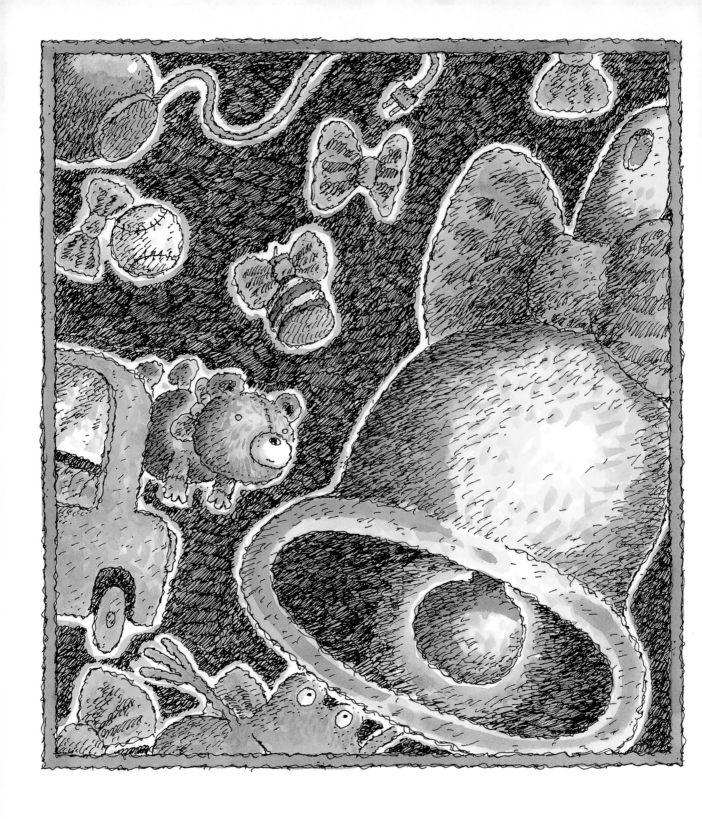

She swallowed the gifts to go with the bows.

She swallowed the bows to tie up the bell
that jingled and jangled and tickled, as well!
I don't know why she swallowed a bell. I wish she'd tell.

Then the old lady needed a treat.
She thought a candy cane would be very sweet.

But when she heard a jolly "Ho! Ho! Ho!"
she knew it was time for her to go.

So she whistled loudly and soon by her side . . .

... was Santa Claus waiting for a ride!